A CHILD PLAY (A REVERIE)

A CHILD PLAY (A REVERIE)

Shahadat Bukhsh

ISBN : 978-93-8022-259-2

First Published, 2015

Published by :

Gennext Publications
23, Main Ansari Road,
Dariyaganj, New Delhi-110002
Ph. : 23282060, 23261060
E-mail: gennext@hotmail.com

Laser Typesetting : Shubham Printers, Delhi

Cataloging in Publication Data—DK
  Courtesy: D.K. Agencies (P) Ltd. <docinfo@dkagencies.com>

Bukhsh, Shahadat, author.
  A child play / Shahadat Bukhsh.
    pages   cm
  Poems.
  ISBN 9789380222592

  1. Indic poetry (English).   I. Title.

DDC 821.92   23

Foreword

The most beautiful saplings sprout out of cracking stony rocks. The darkest clouds have a silver lining that turns to be a splendour lightening the world. The same thing applies to me. My life has been a tragic tale told by the circumstances itself. Thanks to my deceased parents who always inspired me to understand the true meaning of humanity. This very first book of mine; I dedicate this work to my departed parents. Thanks to my little daughters Alvia and Tanvi; my son Mohd. Mohid; my wife Shama Akhtar, My-in-Laws and my family members. Specially, my little angles (Alvia and Tanvi) who are the true sources of inspiration for me.

Acknowledgement

A poet sings of heart. The mind observes the things outwardly. The grasped material echoes in the deep core of heart in its all spiritual sublimity. When the things are extraordinary, they start turning the heart; a lyrical substitute takes place instantly. According to John Keats, it wells up "as naturally as soots to a tree". With the small collection of poetic words, I have mirrored the contemporary society. Humour, satire and irony have been the natural tools of emotional 'expressions' since the time immemorial, found in land of literature in all vividness. My aim is not to malign any one or any type of social set-up. On the contrary, a method of mild humour is adopted in order to gain public attention over "too much" of a system. I have tried in all human humility to present a mild reformative attitude over the traditions, customs and other trivialities of the mundane framework. I apologise for any mistake and seek suitable advice from the experts.

Preface

This collection has been designed as per the requirement of the modern times. Every age covers its entire scenario through literary work. In every world, poetry, due to its innate scheme and structure, has been the source of exposition. There stood a time when the poets of classical age echoed of legends; the romantics out-poured love, beauty and pragmatism; the neo-classical or transitional poets laid emphasis again on "back to nature" and exposed the ugly realities of the contemporariness.

Many things in view, I have tried to focus my attention on the so-called trivialities, sycophancy, fashion, religious bigotry, as well as the pious and kind nature and its agents. I, a humble member of the world-wide society, gift this little creation in the hands of humanity.

Contents

A Child Play

When I sit alone amidst deafening noise,
the soul stirrs me with a sweet voice–
Thou art bonded here with bonds.

My memories sparkle with savour of lyre
We walked on budded carpet of gay grass,
Sang of pleasure, happiness and leisure.
A childran the rivers across!
How sweet were those days! how lovely those days!

The kids we strolled in the summer bare fields,
We marched together with bundles of grass on our head,
We thrilled we tumbled on our little feet,
We laughed, we played, smiled together.
The heavy-winged theives round us lurked,
Our passionate lorn songs broke the gloom ever,
A tired child is filled with pleasure.
How sweet were those days! How lovely those days!
The day was pleasure, and night a treasure,
Of fireflies, Moon, of happiness, of fear.
The cuckoos cooed, from the mango orchards
The ploughmen played in fields the God,
Those sweet coos cured the soul ever!
Birds and beasts endeared the soul.

A group of children runs to a pool,
They play, shrink in jolly mood.
The fishermen drive the fish into net,
Half naked and half wet.
And the chorus of spring that falls!
They yell in love and lofty joy!
How happy were those days ! How lovely are those days!

A Faded Leaf

The milky way fascinate my souls
And star studded sky stretch between the poles.
A ploughman rests least in his bed,
He takes his plough before his bread,
He Sings some hymns, he goes to the field.
He saves the country the nation does build!
A clarion call pours through my ears
It makes me alert a zeal it bears.
A boy hurries home with the bundles of grass,
He paved his way thro, the river across;
Lost in the thoughts of colorful passion,
He hurries next door running with emotion,
The maddening crowd he joins in hope,
And finds the rich in every scope!
The lady's love, he sougnt to win,
But found it hallucination, sin,
He meets a belle with beauty,
Both sportive in fun and gaiety.
He hopes her to meet at the beach
Finds himself puzzled by other man's reach
The flowers, that he brought to her
Like leaves in summer did fast wither;
He finds helpless his love forlorn,
Emotions but a true heart urn–
love Belike feeds on money and matter,
A poor cupid fails, untimely does wither.

The Message

The morn unveils its lovely face,
The splendour falls on the mossy rock,
I enjoy sparrows' chattering grace.
She calls her little one's round the clock.
The breezy call an incense wears,
Brings the message to the oozing eyes,
It thrill's and sweetens my still ears,
My little daughters, naughty and wise,
Chatter the words lovely and dear,
A divine power overflows the sphere,
Those feelings unspoken, but sublime,
Mirror their face, as lake a chime!
Think of God, nature and pleasures
These little ones are but treasures!
O I wish these natures' darlings
Might scatter the words of lofty love,
As on its forehead a bright sun only brings.
The love that floats on water and knows
No grief, no pain, panic, or sorrows,
She strolls in the yard with tottering words,
She echoes like twittering chorus of birds,
I hear a message a worth a thousand lives,
She breaks monotony, the lonliness drives.
Blessed are those who watch the wings of their daughters,
Fly in the hope of love and blessings the gods, farour.
She is the power, she is the guide,
She is the hope, she is the pride.

My Father

Once early in the morn, amidst the mist,
I saw a man with a fork in his fist,
He muttered the divine words with shivering mouth,
He walks slowly slowly towards the south.
Now chanting the hymns with the birds,
The man on his journey fast paved thro' herds,
The morning star, he hailed the cresent moon,
He welcomed all of them very soon.
The dew drops bathed his feet with snow cold,
It smoothered with bitterness but made him bold,
He reached the fields, he salutes the east,
The moon, the star, and the mist.
A splendour unvailed amidst the fog,
Many pyramid-images of fear and snob,
His soul stumbles over for a while
Belike there was a mistake or a vile!

He looked round for his companions
For the Savours for the champions,
And he bent to reap the field of grass,
To bundle the crops to till, to thrash!
He made in bundle prompt of grass,
In abundance of breeze when the hill did pass!
His heart filled with eternal pleasure,
His glowing face, still I treasure
Now a as a grown up I find pleasure
Passing through grasslands and dear river.
No pleasure equals nor does it last,
As the pleasure in memories of the past.
I descend down the ladder of my age
And passes thro' the field on thin serpentine ways.
A wave of pleasure makes me awake
To live a life for its sake.

Unfulfilled Moments

When the night falls, comes the dawn,
The flicker of lights unveils the way,
The thick fog covers the entire lawn,
A traveller sets about shivering and sway
Oh how lovely ! O how pleasant!
When the peopless roads lie asleep,
The rolling wheels crack with nocturnal sense,
Those nearby gardens make a sweep
He treads the stairs with something absence
Oh how lovely ! O how Pleasant !
As if a maiden opens the windowpane,
To watch if there is any difference,
The breeze wraps with sensual pain,
He thinks it all with a daring romance.
Oh how lovely ! O how pleasent!
Birds chatter, kids run and sing,
The splendour falls, the flowers bloom,
The agri-songs, comfort the fetching, of
Bud's eyes have ample room.
Oh how lovely! O how pleasant!
A Miracle happens with a sensuous touch,
She puts her rosy cheeks, makes her balance,
Her quivering lips speak too much,
Listen Oh world the throbbing romance.
Oh how lovely ! O how pleasant!

Ambition

I soar in the seventh zenith
To find if there is peace of mind,
But the echoes of forgotten faces turn behind
Who mock with many a funny gestures,
The ghost of the past, those cruel specters!
It bends my mind below beneath.
Wordsworth's Lucy, or Shelley's sky lark,
Shakespeare's love and Milton's myths,
All them the dust of time sheaths,
But I seek them out amidst the stars,
God hides them safe at distant altars,
Away from sight away from dark!
I wish the faces speak one language—
Of love, of sympathy of courage.
All will relinquish, truth and emotions,
Till I fill my own ambition.

To Say or Not To Say

The winds blow, the heart throbs
The snow capped mountains melt in sun,
The splendour dances nightingale sings,
I sit on the arm chair dozzing, tired.
A knock stirs me at the doors,
She came smiling with lust and love,
How soon flickers the fire of passion!
Beauty adds butterfly a fashion,
Crazy are the heavy winged thieves,
How soon quickens the victorious love!
The beauty moves with gliding strides,
I want to touch her, want to drink the nector of pleasure,
When fire and straw get flamed,
The world is dead while they are alive
How soon, the love-waves arise!
Alas ! They collide with the lofty storms,
The winds of love change and becomes the stormy gust.

Being Human

When the thoughts spring up,
Breaking the heart of stone-headed monsters,
They say how he rhymes.
They charge me of not being a stone-head monster,
Lost in rotten rituals and ceremonies
dancing round the trivial matters,
Ignoring, avoiding fresh airs of new clime.
I stride the path Galilio and Socrates strod,
The differences make me different!
Galilio and Socrates were bound to die under one dire blow,
But me everyone stares at and curses with abuses
Thoughts are not imposed, instead are created.
I strive to be the saviour who revives the thoughts
And leads!
They chase to tread on the foot-prints,
There no sense
For them the most aweful matters become ceremonious!
They murmur the prayers over the dead ass buried long!
They crush my ideas only to live in traditional gutters,
They wear, talismen, emblems, Symbols and engraved marks,
Unmasking their foolish tales with rude thoughts,
They outnumber the forerunners and harbingers–
Chaos, bigotry, bias, sects show them away
They organise a knot of blood and fears,
They boast of being the Hindus, the muslimsall in humane
They are ashamed of calling themselves human.

The Crocodiles

They reach the pinnacle of glory;
In the eyes of heavy-headed monsters,
They start trumpeting the bagpipers
Hissing and gigling the chantings of Phoenix,
They are wrapped with prolife tyre
Numerous and several,
Ill-natured with hallmark of religiosity
People talk together of supernaturals.

They know the laws of Einstein, Darwin and Lemark,
But these Newtons, Edisons, Faradays and Marx
Are only to be read and sent as captive in the almirahs.

They teach the lessons of explorations,
They praise the milky way,
They talk of Mars, Jupitor and cosmic rays–
These items are only to be read and taught.

They bow before the piles of hay,
Their horses stop in the mid way,
They ask like a frostian question,
As if there was something wrong while reading;
The scientific genius to beg excuse,
Not to be punished
From the tortures of the another world,
They teach the taught to be generic
And to follow satanic impressons.

They rue over ill omen, bowing their head down,
Another supports him on the oath of God,
They become celebrity, bowing before
The Gods forbade to bow.

They have an immunity from punishment of rape, loot and arson,
Thank God, they followed God!
They marked a line of their own!
And under the magic line, they stored
Devils, imps, satans and specters in their hearts,
There, under this line lived
An officer, a minister, a doctor, an engineer, a scientist!
The administration, the humanity,
the democracy were second to them.

An officer performs traditional acts,
The traditions go on-the people are killed,
Officer will order to shoot at sight,
So that the traditions are completed–
How can he break the rules of spirituality?
Otherwise he/she will be cursed by God for saken fidelity.
He is a wonderful mixture of duty and religiousity,
Putting a symbol, keeping the talisman.
Democracy needed all
Abraham Lincoln said so.

Once but I, I am alone
Born only to be pooh-poohed, over my turnings deaf ears to
what they say,
To be emotionally, sentimentally crucified!
No one spoke a word
For and against me–
All stared, all gazed, all wondered,
Lastly they went to their hustle and bustle.
There once again I saw the latest an open eyed dream—
Now a scientist is afraid to make any invention, discovery,
or reasearch,
Until he puts a mark of superstition in his heart
And a terror on his face.

Now a scientist is relaxed in such establishments,
He can make experiments tensionless.
He also calls the other scientist of world to join to him–
The other encyclopaedic come
With tradition, the Universel starts his missions
Wastage of time and of money do not account for income tax!
Duty is duty, law is equal to all!

They boast of in their office,
The ceremonies are performed,
This is their previlege!
They claim–
God blessed all men and women,
This is the role of fate, what can a man do,
To them—Milton was wrong who said;
God is great he forgives any sin,
Crime done in the life.
God takes heavy bribery–when they organise,
A ritual
Or a ceremony at a large scale,
Fate rules supereme–
Fate made kings–Caesar and Brutus–
It made Caesar say – Et tu Brute!

Only those deserve hellisn fire
Who go against currupt methods.
Milton, they say, became blind,
As he dared reach God's Heaven,
Murcury cursed him.
They understand God and his trait, for they are well educated,
They go in safari on the beach,
For their safety they hang on Gods,
And they are elite person.
They are anti-provocatives.
They keep their promises in dark and deep.

The Boss Culture

He roared widening his mouth as wide as Atlantic,
And made run the juniors with the speed of rats–
Jumping and frog-hopping,
For they were to salute the *Hindustan Sahib.*
Sahibcracy dominates over the *panditcracy* and *mullacracy*
Unlike the Britishers who conferred the title *sahib,*
All are called sir in *Sahibcracy.*

To be called a sir one must have all
Elephantine trunk.
Under the British rule India found only these sirs:
Sir Syyed, Sir Bankim... Sir Gopal, even the *vilayatis,*
Showed respects them to
These sirs of mother India
Were, those days taken for granted.

We are the best immitators,
We better immitate than the monkeys do
The lion-skinned jackals trumpet with their hollow mouth,
The dignity of the nation
They maintain by yelling yes sir, ok sir thankyou sir.

'Dad' rhymes with 'Bad'
Where there is Dad, the chances of, being bad emerge,
The foolish politicians, officers, and the rich are called 'Dad',

They have turned to be English–
As they are far from,
'Maaf Karna Sahab'
If Danial makes mistake,
He must giggle 'I am sorry, – Sir'
With open mouth, wide as a neighning horse.
Now the sons of Ganga Ram, Abudul and Tota Ram
Like to be called – Dick, Tom and Harry.

II

His duty devides in real and not real,
He contemplates in the whirlpool of to be or not to be, to do or
not to do;
To salute a *gunda mantri* or not with the words that attack his
heart–
Yes sir, ok sir, thank you sir;
To flatter or not the idiot of the idiot box,
To lull him with the word sir is the greatest fodder!
Mother India has ever given birth in numbers!
For such a sir, a man of million of dollars,
Whole earned name, fame and power;
To proport, support, afford and appease to
Yadav Sir, Gupta Sir, Khan Sir and Sharma Sir
Instead of *Ji,* or *Saheb,*
That are out of our culture to be with those, who culminate,
promote;
The Gods who made the world say:
Sir, you are right, God made
You mantriji, adhikari and the boss.

The boss smiles and says, no matter,
And throws a murcury light and they responded,
Yes sir, OK sir, Thankyou sir.

III

Away, away, very far away,
Out of the world of man,
Sits a man, watches the masse's sway–
The human world, the animal world,
And many worlds of all breadth and width–
The ear-deafening words pour into his ears,
He thinks for a lullay of mortal creature's,
But to his wonder, he finds a flattery–
Yes sir, ok sir, thankyou sir!
He peeps downwards– a man flees to the place,
Where sits another man – tied, wide, suited and booted.
He screams upon a junior, calls him a rogue;
The rogue his junior blubs–
Yes sir, ok sir, thankyou sir,
Man for man, but such a difference!
The boss must be a bear, a bloody wolf,
Thinks this innocent child.
The sir is on the visit;
The juniors follow him,
Many smile and suppose themselves the luckist,
For sir turned to them and called out their names;
Name is enough, for the sir called by names.
Some are asked about their family,
They broaden their chest
As sir spoke to them at last!
The sir offers a relief,
Though he helps in brief,
But all mutter to whatever he say–
Yes sir, ok sir, thankyou sir.

When the *sahib,* on the tour
Has gone out to celebrate his fourtieth marriage aniversary,

Leaves behind a note kept under the paper, weight–
Mr. Aman the senior among the juniors will Officiate;
When the man is in-charge,
No one dares ask a question little or large,
The camplainant salutes him high in practice;
The officer in charge hightens his chest,
Rebukes his best,
The complainant only bows down and says–
Yes sir, ok sir, thankyou sir.
The next one in list is Mr. O, O.O.
Who stands to God's PO.
He holds an lucrative portfolio.
He has a duty from welfare to development,
He takes his duty as an enjoyment,
Decorates the office with bouquet, wreaths, flora and fauna,
Becomes a superman, a king at par!
As a lion sits with animals around who says–
'Who will be my minister?
All rush to him open their lips;
The Mr. O. giggles out widening his mouth,
Directs them all to bow down,
All bow and say yes sir, ok sir, thankyou sir.
Now the sir, strolls out for a visit,
Meets many obligations,
Proceeds proud, swift motion!
Others following, like beggars after the rich.
Slams the doors of a school,
The teacher, who is a real preacher,
Trembles, leaves the chair, stands aside with hands bound,
The officer poses in the chair
Like a baboon, a chime in spectales,
The teacher, an image of next to God,
takes the chair with trembling legs;

The officer tells out loudly,
As loud as thunders do.
Idiot, wretched! Thou know not,
Dared you sit ?
Yon will be punished, suspended, terminated?
Crawls the teacher, holds his feet,
Screams the wretched.
You, sit on the ground.
The teacher replies with trembling lips–
Yes sir, ok sir, thankyou sir.
While on the way,
He goes in sway,
All whosoever pass him
Bow down to his say,
He is a cultured Hirnyakashyap,
Whosoever dared is putt a question
Is whipped and jailed.
Once old man spoiled his superiority calling him son;
He is a rascal, he called me son?
How dare he, this poor thundered the boss, old, dirty, rogue?
He even does not know to say,
Yes sir, thankyou sir, ok sir?
Muttered one of the attendants–go to hell. He is Mr. ! O
All stood mute, mum-faced, hushed!

IV

Government orders for investigation of schemes and mega
schemes,
The sir, with his retineue was really there,
Ran the juniors with folded hands–,
A fat rat bell-danced
On seeing so his majesty,
He rolled, he ran, he rolled he ran,

Stumbled in, the way, stood again,
For the boss called his names–
You idiot loafer, scamer, fat valrus— cried the boss;
Yes sir, ok sir, thankyou sir,
Replied the juniors in high chorus.

Now it is an auspicious meeting of the *sahabs;*
They hopped and jumped and sat round the table,
Like the frogs round the pool with their vocal bladders out;
Many ranks, many shapes, but almost the same—
Some were wearing tight snickers,
Some were wearing satin colours,
They were men, not frogs, with diversified wits–
Some were sirs, some were juniors.
Before they could start, they waited for the grand sir,
While waiting they ate, drank Bagpiper.
The grand sir strolled late by three hours,
All of them clapped for he came later,
With his bushy eyebrows, raised high
He spoke in a tone of Scholar–
Sure, sure I am here.
All of them applauded, bowing their heads–
Yes sir, thankyou sir, ok sir.

Now starts the meeting full swings,
The *sahib* orders with elephantine look,
All of them attentive, but a crook turned folded hands–
Excuse me sir, sir please sir;
The hoary–headed *sahib* looks through the spectacles
With a gimmick, ironic smiles orders him to speak–
Sir, please sir, I have brought a gift sir, this is for you sir,
Sir I am enough obedient to you sir,
I remember sir, I remember sir,
Your fourtieth marriage anniversary,

Sir, I remember this this at my deep core of heart sir.
Ok, ok, smiles the big horse,
All clamps with plastic smiles,
Sir, madam our goddess and your goodself God sir,
All are broad-chested as sir receives the gift.

An hour passes, comes a junior,
with folded hands presents a report,
A project report covers budget,
allocation, scams, percentile
Commission and expenses on decorations,
Also he presents the boss's lion's share,
Applauds boss for his public welfare.
All congratulate with
Yes sir, ok sir, thankyou sir.
Servants are paradoxically masters,
And masters are masters, masters can never be servants,
A servant is bound to serve under duly,
Real charm lies, it is a beauty,
The rumour spreads here, comes
The boss, the officer, the sir,
The old, the young, the men, the women,
The physically handicapped,
The weak, the orphan, visully challenged,
All zoom togather,
whisper with wilful eyes,
The *sahib* has a visit.
The teenagers, the first timers
Hear these words–
Sirs, bosses, officers
Think them to be lions, wolves and bears;
They wonder if animals
Do not have identity,
Even they can not be animals,

Who can they be?
One of them rues—they must be aliens
Heralded from the God's land,
So they are the bosses.

Here comes an educated rogue,
He talks of them, to the people gathered round him,
Curious to ask about them.
He tells them, they have to learn to say,
To whatever those 'Big Bosses' say–
Yes sir, ok sir, thankyou sir.

In the nearby hemlet
Some burgalary has made,
The policemen hurry there,
The rustic hide in fear;
A *khaki* man posing self-styled Hitler,
Undermining all wise and fair,
Roars abuses, strikes rod here and there
To frighten them.
He cries such loud,
His juniors waged their tails;
They serve him coffee, chicken roasted plate,
He gallops only to have a fill,
He smokes for the sake of smoke,
He drinks for the sake of drink
Yet he says he is tettoteller.

For many a man chicken a mutton, cigeratte and bribe
Are the part of life,
For he does the duty divine!
Many rush to him, making him,
Asking to offer him the rituals,
Whether he accepts the cocktail,
Or a feast,

He afraid offers pleasures at the best.
A rustic comes,
Gigles out, opening his mouth,
Brings a cot for the *khaki* men
Brushes his shoes, offers him a thousands things.
The men accept the feast
His belly out, he yells loud
And all say— yes sir,
Yes sir, ok sir, thankyou sir.

What do you need further sir?
Flattery soothes boss's ear;
The creamy cocophany makes it clear.
Sits the boss amidst the parasites,
All gaze at him for further services.
Sir yawns, twists his hands,
All are happy,
For sir's yawnings, sir's twisting makes
the way clear
To mutter the words in his praise.
Indians often start with cursing climate;
It starts drizzling after a draught,
Sir feels awkward with the dress he brought,
The rain drops wet his gaberdine,
He moulds, folds, presses with fingers,
All look at him with mercy's petition,
Yawning he says – Damn! It rains!
All giggle out and bows down,
Says –Yes sir, ok sir, thankyou sir.

Comes the winter in Hinterland,
Sir walks around with well gloved hands,
Feels chill, drinks Campa-cola for a relief,
Those who are creamy-cum-chocolate,

Drink Coca Chill at their fascinated will,
To keep aside from stagnated chill.
They live in India, but pose not Indians,
The fashionetta, the Hinglish, the super stars,
The hippo such the modals, the actors,
And all such company men,
Take soft, hard chilled drinks in winter,
They drink champaigne and so on;
Nature ever favours none,
She clutches with frolic and fun,
He falls ill, blames the chill,
Boasts like bombs, they are not ill,
All run out to serve—
Yes sir, ok sir, thankyou sir.

A TV channel with full panel
Calls for the would-be stars
To stride on the herizon of name,
Fame, power, gross embezzlements.
All panelmen are blessed with
Creamy, chubby, choclatty cheeks,
melon belly, thin legs covered under silk.
Their faces are painted, dented and rented,
They are great, greater than the greatest
The great men only are scientists,
Musicians, laureates and artists,
They can not outscore the beauty-pageants
For they make only civilised universe,
Theirs was the asset from nature and self-endeavour.
The show-organisers with toyshops,
Come from heaven defying gods,
And not bowing down to Adam and Eve.
They follow the archrival satan
Now start the competition in all possible pomps!

The newcomers show their arts,
Some are born great says shakespeare,
They perform their arts of dance superior to their masters,
But the hoary-headed the aweful
artificial faces say:
You just missed one step,
You should do this way, you know!
Their way is totally a wrong way,
But they are the masters and dancers,
So the poor, wretched new dancers,
Musician, panting upto death follow them—
Yes sir, ok sir, thankyou sir.
The news channels feel proud to have them with devotion,
The news man asks humbly—
How the actors, actress, models ate, drank, sleep and rest!
She/he feels proud to report!
The moderator pays much attention,
He pours these words on the screen again and again,
They feel happy, for they have a blessings of those,
The newsmen flatter
Yes sir, ok sir, thankyou sir.

Here comes a boss, full rounded of many layered fresh,
A self-styled, unicorn pompey,
Boasting over all the way,
He comes to judge, there is a buzz,
Whatever he decides, in public or private,
All respect him and no one disagrees outwardly,
All silent, all mum faced, all hypnotised,
Breaking the ice, he louds his side,
All show a glow on their face,
He ran almost at par on every face,
He glanced, they whinned,

Yes sir, ok sir, thankyou sir.
The presenter demonstrates the act,
He/she performs at his/her best,
The audiance pray with folded hands,
Their Stars are performing on the stage,
They judge the things,
Make the wings,
The performers press hard
To keep the record at par,
Stay to hear the fate with throbbing heart,
The gang now force the shots,
Speak Hinglish (You just... I mean....
Beautiful... mindblowing... the whole
World Achha hait wow - ooooooo...
The performer understands not
Keeps on saying with panting heart–
Yes sir, sir, ok sir, thankyou sir,
The boss pokes fun under the sun—
Say, you danced like a Bear,
Yes sir, smiles the performer; you danced like a cat,
Thankyou sir, you danced like grosshopper,
Ok sir, smiles the performer;
For they all spoke English,
They found abuse, some kind of blessings,
provided they must be spoken in English.

A decorated star comes on the stage
Proud and pays a homage,
They start barking with pursing lips,
Create the sound, wow. wow,
Just calling foxes and rabbits,
The well-fed chicken-faced stars–
Jump on the stage blowing hips–

Make gestures made by celebs
An aweful lady of the gang,
Makes a big bang,
Fires a shot of wow
Wow-wows she, O' weeps for kissing,
The hero of her dream,
The hero consoles her,
Gives a hug, licks her rolling tears,
Giggles out the lady with swollen chest,
Peeps inside if there is some mistake,
If she got an electric touch,
Was it less or at least much?
The beau intentionally fish out the matter formally,
Yet he yells in the jackal tone,
Takes, respons, from the lady—
Throwing hot balloons she cries—
Yes sir, ok sir, thankyou sir

V

Killers the worldover, are for slaughters,
Duty eats up moral and manners,
Bloodshed Occupancy, land-slide victory,
All are birth right of militancy
They shout holding guns in their hands,
They cry hateful words clash in bands,
They create the voices of broken drum;
Mother nature shivers, holds mum,
When comes no man's land
There roars a big band
Frightening birds, animals and butrerflies;
How wise the lessons of enmity the killers find—
Every thing is sure to be murdered,

Men women children are not barred,
A true patriot is one, who, for the sake of country,
loves all outside the LoC
Albert Einstein condemned nationalism for it is measles,
Bernard Shaw pooh-phood over the soldiers,
These were not patriot they say,
They had no country as their own,
Serving is the art of murdering men;
Scholars, writers and scientists in vain.
A bad man must have
A mind versed with hatred and revange...
Wars are created, battels were fought,
Under ideals taught to soldiers and Generals—
Humanity must be maintained,
Patrotism sure to be retained.

VI

To talk of *babudom*
is to talk of kingdom
For only *babus* are allocated with super stars;
A high school pass twists at par,
A needy enters his *durbar,*
Saluting the wretched seeks his grace,
Vulture-eyed *babu* contorts his face,
A hoary-headed boss peeps through the glass
Sitting from another wall,
Waits if the *babu* performs well
The duty branded with him must not fail—
The visitor, a public man with scholarly uniform,
Frightened, afraid with inferiority complex,
Celebrates the festival of give and take,
Giggles over the issue, requests for review,
The *babu* with the dignity of a king

Takes the pin,
Starts scratching his red teeth,
The visitor understands pushes money into his hands,
Begins the market of give and take,
Smiles the *babu* saying venomously,
" I am the best,
I do my best",
The visitor sings in low tone–
Yes sir, O.k. sir, thankyou sir.

VII

Democracy needs hypocrisy,
Hypocracy hatches *gundacracy;*
Politics is the easiest game,
Only the tricky, the rich play,
For he, who is moneyed, is surely wise,
For a politician wisdom comes,
Only when he is enhanced
With the qualities of psycophancy.

Democracy a rule of the people–
For the people and by the people
Turns into tyraany of the people,
For the people and by the people.
The songs of patriotic note
Must be played to get vote.
The leaders come out of their *hamams*.
For planning they come to Delhi
"A Tokyo" does not suit them.
The Democrates speak as high as stars,
Promise every thing these political liars,
Democracy needs sacrifice,
They don't notice,

These parasites work as silent killers
Divide and rule and scratches their whiskers,
They water the futile ground:
Anexity, hunger, loot and arson,
Rape, scam, murder and plunder.

My countrymen, land me your ears, says a leader,
I have come to tell the scams, not the scammers,
All but my party belongs to the school of scandals,
We share the crazy *salad* of hate, devide and rule,
No matter we ride on a horse or a mule,
But I swear with God divine,
We will open not universities, but only auditoriums
O people, I swear in the name of God,
There will no longer be a froud,
We will allow no communal riots,
Now we will allow no more fights,
Only if you vote for me.
I prostrate before you on my knee,
Our party is only committed to make
Mandir, masjid, for India's sake,
No matter China, America, England, Germany–
Explore, invent, investigate, educate,
advance towards the moon,
Confirms a new world soon,
Here we are proud to be Hindus,
We are proud to be Muslims,
We are not proud to be a Hercules
Of power, love and unity,
We are proud of our cultures,
That are full of many creatures,
Our progress zoom round the fables of prayer, ritual and
supernatural,
I pledge, my party will find more and more,

Make our country a hub of followers
Of religion and morality.
He waves his hands
He asks the bands.
If they satisfy his mode of devastation,
To keep the country out of frustruation, of progress,
in science, astronomy, geography and cosmology;
To live in peace one needs
Not the progressive attitude, one must have a biased aptitude—
of selfish–love, not human-love.

The maddenning crowd
With the deafening sound
Cry in versioned English
Yes sir, ok sir, thankyou Sir.

An Elegy to Age

People call him uncle,
Uncle denotes a non-visionary;
Has been coined in modern dictionary.
The aged get a shock,
When he is called uncle,
No matter which age or sphere,
In the depth of glamour,
Uncle emerged with fun and laughter—
Hello uncle, sorry uncle, how do you do uncle!
Here comes a prufrock,
Head shining like a rock,
Makes an approach
Like a cockroach,
Throws his image of a hero, practically a total zero,
Handshakes a rustic,
with a smile made of plastic—
Hello uncle, sorry uncle, how do you do uncle!
They invented uncles,
For them age "No bar", caste no bar,
They wear no beard, mustaches,
Hello uncle, sorry uncle, how do you do uncle!
Uncle is dirty blot,
On the face muzzled with the grace!

Works this weapon of disgrace so swift!
A male may stay alive, a female swoons dead,
If she hears to be called Aunty,
She gets heart stroke, lies in the bed,
You say not—
Hello Aunty, Sorry Aunty, How do you do Aunty.

Never ask a woman's age,
Make her happy, win her favour, call her underage,
Age can not wither away Cleopatra,
Babies cry at painted faces,
They yell.
Travelling makes a comfortable zone—
Many uncles make wait for beauty,
Craving salad eye a belle.
Make a gesture of heart, simple and bread,
Shock, the belle mocks.
The red zone starts, when a contemporary calls
Hello uncle.
A lady talks of birth, marriage, parentage,
Before greetings she tells about her age.

An adolscent daughter sits behind
Giggles, how early she got married!
She was thirteen.
Men at fifty, get more crafty,
Swimming mid way find difficult to make a hey,
They try utmost all ways;
Remove out mustaches, undermine, culture,
Become a cholate-faced sculptor,
Grey hair is the call of grey age,
Eliot's Prufrock confessed, "I grow old I grow Old".
They claim to be too young, too bold,
Get irked, frown upon those who call them

Hello uncle.

A Lady wept,
Passersby consoled, yet she wept
Tear rolled down her cheeks
Oh she cried, do not call me aunty, please.
The hypocrite butter.
She looks of thirty, feels very happy, when youngsters call,
Hello *bhabhi*,
They whole-heartedly make a prayer,
Pray to getback age and lustre;

The Miracles

They believe the miracle, not the humors,
They nouris' the dead, not the living
Many, Many flock togather
To get miracles handy and forever.
Kremlin got them crushed, China got these
smashed and hence
Stride on the horizon of aerospace.
Science discards fusion, when there is confusion,
Always there stands a way,
For rome was not built in a day.

Malnourished babies crawl in the huts,
Run to grab, gobble anything they have,
Ludicrous, unhygienic, a lively skelton!
The well-nourished tread on the ground, an image of lion hunters!

Some are crushed, with deadly disease,
Others are deprived of human touch,
They move their toyshop place to place,
Charge the innocuous batteries with bigotry,
The godman sits on the judgement seat,
In the holy tower; makes a sectarian call,
Surely religion, heresay, curse, blessing fall on all, who
knowingly are unable to treat
The clarion call for pouring money and matter.
The ignorant, the educated are looted,
Their hard-earned legacy goes in vain,
They plung, into the mud.

The Festivals

A little girl sits huddled, at the corner of the house;
Her heart starts pounding, even at the moving of a mouse.
Thinks, if someone brings a message of the blood outrage;
A phone call, make stunned all,
A hush-hush chating makes upset all,
A nearby place again in the grip of riot,
Rioters and riot-victims;
Curfew has been imposed, no one comes.
Festivals of peace, love and devotion,
harmony and enjoyment,
Turned into hell.
The little girl wonders, how people are venomised!
To pour hatred, fear, violent intentions.

Festivals, rituals, celebrations,
Are now faithless ego demonstrations.
She peeps out of the window.
Man is afraid of man.
They are not afraid of lions, wolves and tigers.
Man has become more deadlier.
Now man wears - Bigotry, hatred and revange in hallucinated

mind,
Frowns upon one another with ideas unkind.
At another place, sits a group of persons,
Whispering words of ill-will.
The others pass, with throbbing hearts almost dead.
Hark! the little one sees dangers to be found,
Men are equipped with the weapons of hate.
Festivals are made for love, joy and pleasure;
Bring us closer, nearer and nearer.
It seems, the things right once upon a time
Now have changed into another rhyme,
One man's festivals was other man's interval,
Every one shared this with joy and flavour,
The festivals bore no blame of caste, creed or colour,
One man's festival was another's joy.
The life, flew with flying colours,
Festival was full of love and laughter.
Alas! she thinks, how faded the colours?
Now a festival, frightens others,
The intoxicated mass encroaches upon everywhere,
Crying, hooping, deafening, beating,
Yelling, dancing, frowning and sweating.

Here comes a group dipped wholly in religious gaberdine.
Law and men can not oppose to whatever they propose.
Right to freedom makes the way,
They are free to do whatever they may.
Their croony minds outlaws all, only they shine,
They can pollute, they can yell,
The earth shivers, the quakes are created,
When the high festivities are displayed.
Gods are happy, the sky feels fears,
Law remains unsound.

II

The little girl steps further out,
She notes them fight every way stout,
This is mine,
They fight, as the nomads fought,
Over the piece of flash they brought,
To usurp, to gallop, to have a bite;
Authorities move, examine the conditions
Curfew is imposed, no one is allowed,
Enquiry installed, courts look active,
Newspaper relish the *masala,*
Blood-shed takes place,
Humanity becomes wild, society of wolves!
Ready to kill one another
Curfew declared, no one dared.
Left were cracks, differences, fear and tears!
The fate of country, the fate of people is thrown
Under the weight of hate and unrest.

III

The little one makes hurried steps
To find out the judements.
The victims come, wailing out of grief
To find high assurances and dictates:
"We will set an enquiry, we will set an enquiry
Besides this, no more querry, no more querry"
Some are taken into custody.
Judgement delayed is judgement denied.

The little one hopes "good days" for humanity,
Let justice be done, though the heavens may fall!
This little one wishes a farewell to all.
No more hatred, no more strife, no more wail,
Let peace, love, harmony in everyone prevail.

 A Child Play

Bird

One day, I was sitting on my doorway,
The bird of my heart, suddenly had a flight
Crossed the seventh zenith.
Wandering, every where, got down on hemisphere.
Met a wonton "apsara".
I got whirlled, in my mind.
Oh! you, you the goddess of heaven!
Said she, "Love knows no heaven, no hell,".
I am your love lorn creature.
My soul cried, warned me.
"O wretched!
Thy life must be clean.
She came to mar your.
Emotions collided against realism–
"What truth, What lie in love?".
"No, no, Heer-Ranjha, Manu-Shraddha.
Became the pinnacle, made glory of love".
She stood before me, a statue
Of the meuseum of Madam Tushad.
Waiting for my reply,
Love is worship, no bondage,
She whinned.
Everywhere, on leaflets of Daffodils

Flowers have no caste, religion or region.
The tide of emotions broke the wall.
In a moment, I was shackeled in love,
Lust overpowered.
'Oh, what an awaful nightmare!
I woke up, found me surrounded with cold waters
Of lonliness,
Remained her dust,
Like a beaten dog, a robbed man,
returned to house.
The door of my house lie opened.

The Followers

I sensed something into nothing
"Perhaps" a gust of wind or,
A sound of someone's passing.
whatever!
My heart starts pounding,
The stormy winds make the stable-wall stir,
I alone, hopeless like a broken pot,
Am mocked by the fate-line of my hands;
A line that never fallowed,
Searched its own way, away from bands'.
I ask astonishingly; "If a line makes a way?"
My soul cried,
Thou art coward,
These were the follwers,
Corruption, castism, superstitions and injustice,
Science, humanity, and civilisation,
Heralded with hope and beauty.
The birds sang in praise of all,
A sweet smile played on the beautiful coral lips!
Love, beauty, romance in flowers,
filled the music in naturals.

Before all these fruits come to mellowness
There encroached a devil afraid worried and sad.

Mind and heart sought rest,
A black shadow covered the whole universe,
With swords, daggers, and deadly cannons—
"Today all will finish, humanity will pay,
love will be destroyed,
Every where chaos, deadly scences, humanity is ending.
Love, humanity, brotherhood and sympathy
were left only blind followers,
No one spoke a word,
Who spoke against this "line"
Were crushed under elephantine feet,
Socrates, Galilio, Gandhi and Lincoln
Doomed to suffer badly for they
Searched a new line.